First published in the United States, Great Britain, Canada,
Australia, and New Zealand in 1988 by North-South Books,
an imprint of Nord-Süd Verlag AG, Gossau Zürich, Switzerland.
First paperback edition published in 1997.
Distributed in the United States by North-South Books Inc., New York.

Library of Congress Cataloging-in-Publication Data
Snow White and Rose Red/Jacob and Wilhelm Grimm;
retold and illustrated by Bernadette Watts.
Summary: A bear, befriended by two sisters during the winter,
returns one day to reward them royally for their kindness.
[1. Fairy tales. 2. Folklore—Germany.] I. Grimm, Jacob, 1785-1863.
II. Grimm, Wilhelm, 1786-1859. III. Watts, Bernadette, ill.
PZ8.S416   1988   87-72036 / AC

A CIP catalogue record for this book is available from The British Library.

ISBN 1-55858-054-9 (trade binding)
1 3 5 7 9 TB 10 8 6 4 2
ISBN 1-55858-696-2 (paperback)
1 3 5 7 9 PB 10 8 6 4 2
Printed in Belgium

For more information about our books, and the authors and artists
who create them, visit our web site: http://www.northsouth.com

Jacob and Wilhelm Grimm

Snow White and Rose Red

Retold and Illustrated by Bernadette Watts

North-South Books

Once upon a time there was a poor widow who lived in a lonely cottage. In the garden surrounding the cottage stood two little rose trees; one had white roses, the other red.

The widow had two daughters. One was pale and fair like the white roses; the other was rosy-cheeked like the red roses. They were good girls, always busy and cheerful. But Snow White was quieter and gentler than Rose Red. Rose Red was a lively girl who loved to run through the fields and the forest, while Snow White preferred to stay at home with their mother, helping her with the chores or reading to her when there was nothing else to do.

The two children were very fond of each other. When Snow White said, "We will never leave each other," Rose Red always answered, "Never, so long as we live." Their mother often said, "Whatever one has, she always shares with her sister."

When the two sisters went to gather strawberries in the forest, the animals did not harm them and instead came up to them. The little hares ate cabbage leaves from their hands, the deer grazed at their feet while the stags leapt about, and all through the forest the birds sang for them.

Snow White and Rose Red kept the cottage clean and tidy. It was so neat, it was a pleasure to peep inside it. In the summer Rose Red cared for the house, and every morning she put a rose from each tree by her mother's bed before she woke. In the winter Snow White kindled the fire and kept the brass kettle on the hob full. The kettle was polished so finely it shone like gold.

In the evening, when the snow began to fall, the mother would say, "Snow White, please bolt the door." Then they would sit around the fire and the mother would put on her spectacles and read aloud from a book of old fairy tales while the two girls listened eagerly.

Their pet lamb would sleep on the floor and a white dove would sleep on a perch with its head tucked under its wing.

One evening, as they sat together cosily, there was a heavy knock at the door. The mother said, "Quick, Rose Red, open the door, it must be a traveler seeking shelter."

Rose Red drew back the bolt, expecting to find a poor man. Instead she found a huge bear as tall and as wide as the doorway!

Rose Red screamed and sprang back, the lamb bleated, the dove fluttered, and Snow White hid under her bed.

But the bear spoke gently, "Do not be afraid, I will not hurt you. I am half-frozen and only want to warm myself by your fire."

"Poor bear," said the mother, "Lie down on the hearth, but take care not to burn your coat. Snow White! Rose Red! Come out, the bear will do you no harm. He means well."

The girls crept out, then the lamb and the dove drew nearer.

The bear said, "Here children, please brush the snow off my coat." So they fetched the broom and swept him clean; then he stretched himself out by the glowing logs, growling contentedly.

Soon the children were playing tricks on their guest. They tugged his hair, put their feet on his back and rolled him about. The bear took it all in fun and when they were too rough only growled.

Leave me alone children!
Snow White and Rose Red
Would you beat your lover dead?

At bedtime the kind mother said, "You can sleep by the embers, and be sheltered from the bad weather." At daybreak the two children let him out, and he trotted off into the snowy forest.

Then the bear came every evening at the same time, stretched out by the hearth, and let the children play with him. They all became such good friends that the door was never fastened at night until the bear had arrived.

When spring came and all the world was green again, the bear said to Snow White one morning, "Now I must go away and cannot come back till the end of summer."

"Where are you going, dear bear?" asked Snow White.

"I must go into the forest and guard my treasures from the wicked dwarfs. In winter, when the earth is frozen hard, they have to stay underground because they cannot dig themselves out. But now that the sun has warmed the earth, they will soon come out to pry and steal. Whatever they steal they hide deep in their caves."

Snow White was sad to see the bear go. As she unbolted the door for him, and he was hurrying out, a strange thing happened. He caught his fur on the bolt and a patch was torn away; and it seemed to Snow White as if gold gleamed through the place where the hair had been torn away.

The bear quickly disappeared into the deep forest.

A few days later the mother sent her daughters into the forest to gather kindling. There they found a great fallen tree. Close by the trunk something was furiously hopping back and forth, but they could not see what it was. They tip-toed nearer and saw a dwarf with an old crinkled face and a snow-white beard a yard long. The end of the beard was caught in the tree, and the dwarf was jumping about in a terrible temper, unable to escape.

He glared furiously at the girls and shouted out: "Why do you stand and stare? Come here and help me!"

"What are you doing?" asked Rose Red.

"You stupid, nosy fool!" retorted the dwarf. "I was splitting the tree to cut logs for cooking. I had just driven in the wedge and everything was going well, but suddenly the wedge sprang out again and the tree snapped shut and trapped my beautiful white beard. Now I cannot get away, and you horrid creatures stand there laughing at my misfortune!"

The children tried very hard, but could not pull the beard out. "I will run and fetch someone!" said Rose Red.

"Idiot!" shouted the dwarf. "Why fetch anyone? You are already two too many; think of something else!"

"Don't be impatient," said Snow White kindly. "I will help you." She took her scissors out of her pocket and snipped off the end of the beard.

As soon as he was free the dwarf seized a bag filled with gold which lay half-hidden among the treeroots, swung it over his crooked back, and slunk away, grumbling to himself, "Beastly children, to cut off a piece of my fine beard. Bad luck to you!"

Some days later Snow White and Rose Red went to the river to catch fish. Near the water they saw something that looked like a large grasshopper jumping up and down, as if it was going to dive in. They ran up and found it was the dwarf. "What are you up to now?" asked Rose Red. " Surely you don't want to go into the water?"

"I am not a fool," shouted the rude little dwarf. "Can't you see that huge fish is pulling me in?"

He had been sitting on the bank fishing when the wind had tangled his beard in the fishline. A moment later a big fish took a bite and the little man was not strong enough to land it. He held onto reeds and rushes, for the fish was slowly but surely dragging him into the rushing water.

The girls had arrived just in time. They held him tight and tried to free his beard, but it was so tangled in the line that once again Snow White took her scissors and snipped part of it off.

The dwarf was furious and screamed out, "Is that polite, you toadstools, to disfigure a man's face? First you snip off the end of my beard, and now you have cut off the best part! I cannot be seen! Get out of my way!"

Then he snatched up a sack of pearls concealed among the rushes and quickly dragged it away, disappearing behind a stone.

Some time later the mother sent the two children to the village to buy provisions. Their way wound across heathland scattered with rocks. There they spied a huge bird in the sky soaring in slow circles. It flew down and settled on a rock not far off. Immediately they heard a pitiful scream. They hurried to the rock and once again saw the little dwarf, who was caught in the bird's talons.

The kind children grasped the little dwarf tightly and struggled with the bird until at last it let go of its prey. The dwarf recovered from his dreadful fright and then shouted angrily at the girls, "Couldn't you have been more careful? Look at my best brown coat, it has been all torn, you clumsy creatures!"

He then picked up a bag full of precious stones and slipped under a rock into the entrance to his cave. The girls went on their way and did their shopping in the village.

In the evening the children were returning home across the heath, when they suddenly came across the little dwarf again. He had emptied out the bag of precious stones in a secret spot, thinking no one would come that way. The last rays of sun shone upon the beautiful jewels; they glittered so brightly the children were amazed.

"What are you staring at?" shouted the dwarf, jumping to his feet. His face turned copper-red with rage.

He was still cursing when the three heard a loud growling and a huge bear lumbered towards them out of the forest. The terrified dwarf turned to run but before he could escape into his cave the bear was upon him. Shaking with fear the dwarf begged, "Dear Mr. Bear, spare me. I will give you all my treasures – look at all these beautiful jewels! Let me live, I would not make much of a meal for you. Come, take these two wicked girls, they are plump and tender!"

The bear took no notice and knocked the dwarf to the ground with one blow from his great paw. The girls had run away, but the bear called to them, "Rose Red, Snow White! Do not be afraid; wait and I will come with you!"

Then the sisters recognized the bear's voice and waited. When he approached them, his bearskin suddenly fell off, and there stood a handsome young man, dressed in clothes made of gold.

"I am a King's son," he said, "and I was under a spell, cast by that wicked dwarf, who had stolen my treasures. I was forced to roam the forest as a wild bear until I was freed by his death. Now he has received his punishment."

When Snow White grew up she married the handsome prince, and Rose Red married his brother. The old mother came to their magnificent castle and lived there peacefully and happily to the end of her days. She took the two rose trees with her and planted them by her window, and every year they bore beautiful roses, white and red.